Leo the Late Bloomer

BY ROBERT KRAUS • PICTURES BY JOSE ARUEGO

Windmill Books

New York

Leo the Late Bloomer

Text copyright © 1971 by Robert Kraus

Illustrations copyright © 1971 by José Aruego

All rights reserved. No part of this book may be used or reproduced in any manner whatsoever without written permission except in the case of brief quotations embodied in critical articles and reviews. Manufactured in China. For information address HarperCollins Children's Books, a division of HarperCollins Publishers, 10 East 53rd Street, New York, NY 10022.   www.harperchildrens.com

LC Number 70-159154

ISBN 0-87807-042-7

ISBN 0-87807-043-5 (lib. bdg.)

ISBN 0-06-443348-X (pbk.)

09 10 11 12 13 SCP 20 19 18 17 16 15 14

'Windmill Books' and the colophon
accompanying it are a trademark of
Windmill Books, Inc., registered in
the United States Patent Office.
Published by Windmill Books, Inc.
Distributed by HarperCollins Publishers.

For Ken Dewey

J. A.

For Pamela, Bruce
and Billy

R. K.

Leo couldn't do anything right.

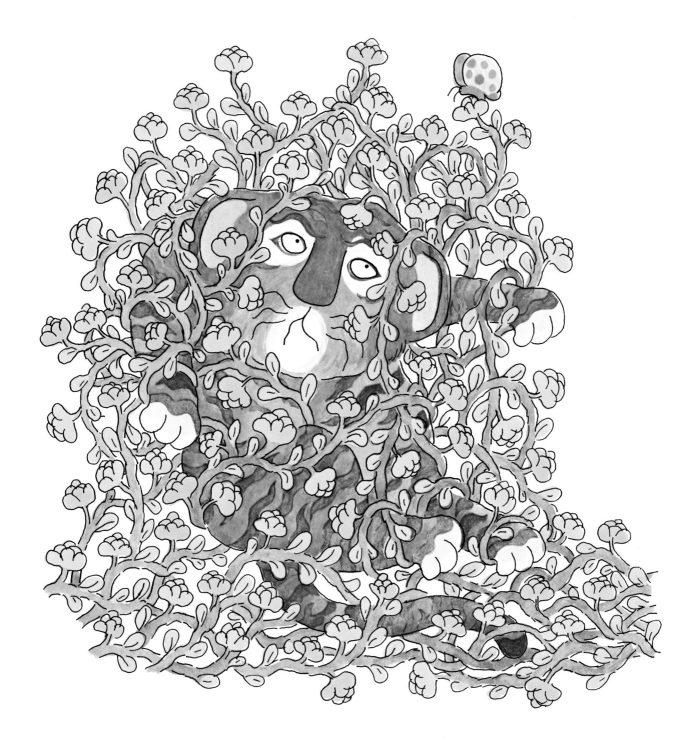

He couldn't read.

He couldn't write.

owl
Elephant
Snake
Plover
Crocodile

He couldn't draw.

He was a sloppy eater.

And, he never said a word.

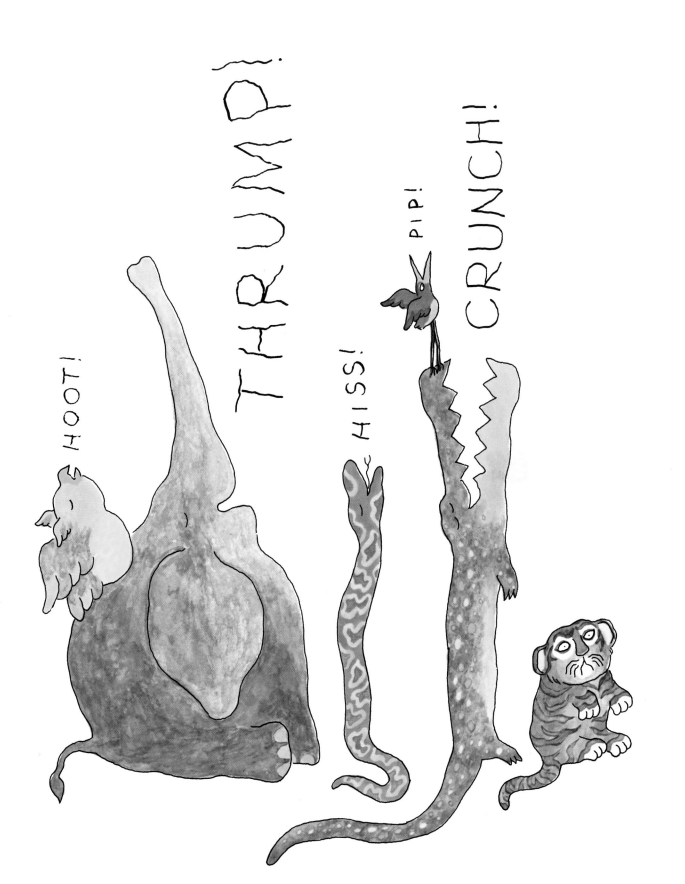

"What's the matter with Leo?"
asked Leo's father.
"Nothing," said Leo's mother.
"Leo is just a late bloomer."
"Better late than never," thought Leo's father.

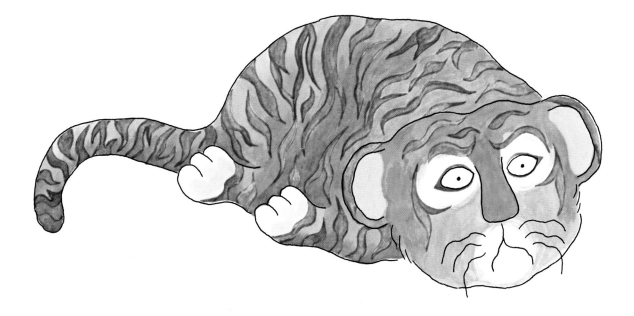

Every day Leo's father watched him
for signs of blooming.

And every night Leo's father watched him
for signs of blooming.

"Are you sure Leo's a bloomer?"
asked Leo's father.
"Patience," said Leo's mother.
"A watched bloomer doesn't bloom."

So Leo's father watched television
instead of Leo.

The snows came.
Leo's father wasn't watching.
But Leo still wasn't blooming.

The trees budded.
Leo's father wasn't watching.
But Leo still wasn't blooming.

Then one day,
in his own good time,
Leo bloomed!

He could read!

He could write!

He could draw!

He ate neatly!

He also spoke.
And it wasn't just a word.
It was a whole sentence.
And that sentence was...

"I made it!"